LUCK BE THE LADIES

A GROUP X CASE STORY

J. A. BOUMA

LUCK BE THE LADIES

Ah, Sin City. The City of Lights (along with Paris), the City that Never Sleeps (along with New York), the City of Second Chances (yeah, right!)

How about the Marriage Capital of the World. Or the Entertainment Capital of the World. More like the Gambling Capital of the World, especially when Numero Siete was involved, the number of Lady Luck.

Except for when it wasn't.

Because Lucky Seven wasn't so lucky for the prostitute who was missing an arm and a leg. Irony of ironies, since this was Vegas. Seven was sort of a Vegas totem for Lady Luck making an appearance.

Not for Kiki Cormorant.

Not sure if that was her real name or stage name—or perhaps street name, given her chosen occupation.

But it was a doozie! Because a cormorant is a kind of sea bird, which was a bit ironic since I was standing in basically a hydrated desert, the Great State of Nevada seeing fit to pump umpteen gallons of water from Lake Mead, which gets its water from the Colorado River. Ninety percent of it, actually. Which, if I were Colorado, I'd have a conniption over, demanding payments from here to Sunday.

Anyway, Kiki, who was missing an arm and a leg—both, actually, in keeping with the familiar pattern that had dragged my backside and my partner Gina Anderson three-quarters of the way across the United States.

Cost her nothing to lose her limbs, too, other than being in the wrong place at the wrong time. Which was working the Vegas Strip, along with the rest of her sisters of the street-corner short shorts waiting for the next John looking for a good time. Would normally add *or gal looking for a good time*, but this was the mid-2000s, and that really wasn't a thing yet. At least not publicly. Obergefell was another decade way, although *Ellen* certainly did enough to push the needle forward, along with *Will & Grace*.

Anyhoo, my partner and I were brought in when it was clear seven dead prostitutes wasn't a rounding error. Apparently, six wasn't so bad, but seven—that was enough to make the sex workers unionize. Which was not good business for the pimps that worked in the gutters running under Sin City.

Certainly wasn't good for Sin City itself; serial killers tend to dampen the mood, not to mention tourist traffic, which was the city's primo economic driver. Nothing like the Almighty Dollar to kick Uncle Sam's keister into gear. After all, dollars sing, and Luck Be a Seventh-Dead Lady Tonight was the tune.

It was Vegas, after all. They had their superstitions like any other joint across the Fifty-Nifty United States.

So there we were, having just rolled up in our FBI-issued Chevy Suburban (black, of course) to Clark County Rifle-Pistol Center & RV Park. A sad joint planted well outside the glitzy glamor of the Strip. Flat and dry, filled with nothing but rocks and those tumbly tumbleweeds I always thought really weren't a thing. Nope. They're a thing, alright. Sometimes called a wind witch, but really the skeleton of a Russian thistle, so named after the Russian immigrants who imported it in seeds for wheat and other crops.

And there we were, with said tumbleweeds, the heat slapping us in the face hoofing it through a part of Vegas no one in their right mind would touch.

Out of sight, out of mind.

Pretty well summarized the plight of most of humanity. Especially prostitutes caught in the web of what was later determined to be a serial killer.

How'd we figure that? Well, the female torso missing both her arms and legs pretty well clued us in. Especially since that matched the MO of six other broads discovered at various parts around the City of Lights.

Luck be the ladies, no way.

First one was discovered inside a big dumpster behind Mickey Ds filled with leftover frying old. Scared the pimply faced high schooler crapless when he opened the side door to deposit his load—when a brunette's head flopped out. In fact, word on the street was that actually he did lose his crap, but I don't peddle in rumors. What matters is that the broad set the stage for the future.

No arms, no legs.

Same for the second victim, discovered under an I-15 overpass. Victim Three turned up in a Burger King garbage dump (this time a retired granny nearly lost her dentures taking out the morning trash). At least the perp had upgraded from the Golden Arches to the Home of the Whopper, but still. Not good for Sin City business. The Fourth was found by some hikers in Calico Basin, which was when it all started to register on the Las Vegas Metropolitan Police Department's radar.

One dead night walker was nothing. Two was business, even given the nature of the crimes. Three, now that was a little less than a rounding error for them type. And, given the unusual markings of the victims (IOW, missing limbs), it was a lot more paperwork than it was worth. But four— well, now that couldn't be ignored.

Especially when Vic Five was found closer to home floating face-first in the Bellagio fountain. Took the cheese-cake, that sure did!

The real zinger was Numero Seis lying in Caesar's Palace when the cleaning crew came to fluff the pillows. Not that prostitutes didn't frequent the joint. Was right bad for business. Which should have piqued the Feds interest (dollars sing, and Luck Be a Seventh-Dead Lady Tonight was the tune, remember?) but not yet.

Not until Lucky Seven.

The perp had moved outside the Strip, much to the relief of LVMPD. Except there was a tiny detail they weren't expecting on that last one.

Lucky Seven wasn't just any victim. She was the major's cousin's daughter.

How's that for a made-for-streaming turn of things?

So, if dollars sing, family makes the world go round.

Or is it, dollars make the world go round and family sings?

Not sure on either front.

Either way, once it was on the mayor's radar—really and truly—well, there wasn't stopping the wheels of government intervention from turning.

And turn they did, until they resulted in me and Gina flying 2089 miles—exactly. I counted. Needed to in order to prep myself for the cross-country jaunt 34,000 miles above the surface of Earth. Because nothing but the most urgent of cases would get me flying—especially coach. And especially American Airlines! Couldn't the Bureau have at least put us up with Delta? Even United would have been better than that disaster of an airline. After all, it was their Flight

11 that took down the Twin Towers. And we all know what happened after that.

But we'd made it—thanks to the beverage cart and a bottle of Xanax. The latter for Gina and the former for me, a few bottles of Altos Las Hormigas Malbec to keep me from freaking out, given my aerophobia. Yeah, didn't exactly disclose that one to Agent Pendergast when I joined the Bureau. But I'd managed well enough.

And now we were staring at a torso that reminded me of one of my favorite children's shows, *Today's Special*.

Each night, Jodie the department store display builder would show up with Jeff the Mannequin, lugging his lifeless body inside. And every night, without fail, Muffy the Mouse would say those magical words to bring him to life: *'hocus pocus alimagocus!'*

Loved that show. The only one I and my fellow orphans were allowed to watch in that wretched Virginia orphanage.

And there was Kiki, reminding me of a mannequin without its limbs. Body lifeless, less than human. A shadow of humanity that was waiting for Muffy to bring it to life— or back to life, as was this case.

"I think I'm gonna be sick..." Gina moaned.

I sighed and nodded. "Does take the cheesecake, don't it?"

"Don't you mean cake?"

"Nope. Cheesecake. Hate them kind. Especially that restaurant chain."

"The Cheesecake Factory?"

"Bingo."

"Who doesn't like The Cheesecake Factory? They've got more than two-hundred different kinds of dishes. Their Cajun Jambalaya Pasta is the bomb!"

She turned to me, eyes wide with interest. "You don't

think they've got one of those in these parts, do you? I could really go for that—"

"Nope."

"Nope? What nope?"

"We got four of them," one of the agents crooned from his notepad. The tall one, with a wicked comb-over that made him look like Ron Jeremy, the infamous '80s porn star. Not that I'd know anything about that sort of thing. Saw him on MTV's *The Surreal Life*. Once. A long time ago.

Anyhoo, back to Agent Comb-over. Kenny Garafalo. Yes, you heard right. Kenny G. Which sort of fit, with that rumpled off-the-rack suit. Probably J.C. Pennys. Not that I'm judging or anything. Brooks Brothers for me. Which sort of smacked DC cliché, but whatever.

"Really, where?" Gina shrieked, turning to Kenny G with interest.

"Nope," I insisted. Had to rein it in, pronto!

"For the love…"

"Where are the limbs?" I asked, changing the subject pronto.

Kenny shoved his pencil behind his ear, then jerked a finger thataway before saying, "Thataway."

So thataway I went, Gina throwing up a sigh but tagging along.

Lined with upscale casino hotels, the neon-soaked Strip is quintessential Las Vegas, or so Wikipedia told me before we left DC. Had never been. Never wanted to go, thanks to this case straight from hot Hades. But getting a looksee on our way to the crime scene, the upstart online brain sure was correctamundo.

You've got a myriad of gambling floors, vast hotel complexes housing a variety of shops, restaurants—the low-end Subway joint to high-end, hundred–dollar oyster bars for muckety-mucks making far more than government wage. Then there are all the performance venues for music, comedy and circus acts—with high wires and elephants, Seinfeld and Celine Dion.

My favorite so far was the soaring, choreographed Fountains of Bellagio and the High Roller observation wheel.

But where we were wasn't that. Not by a mile. In fact, we were about twenty miles north of the Strip, which led to a surprising change of scenery.

Because Clark County Rifle-Pistol Center & RV Park ain't the Strip, that's for sure. Wasn't even sure I'd call it an RV *park*, on account there weren't no trees. Just a dry desert wasteland wilderness, something my people were intimately familiar with.

I'm Jewish, see. Or Messianic, having realized Yeshua the Nazarene was the long-promised Messiah, the One whom my people had hung their yarmulkes on and Yahweh had promised from the beginning. So the wilderness was in my blood, given my ancestor's wanderings and all.

Anyhoo, back to Clark County Rifle-Pistol Center & RV Park, which was nestled at the base of a peaking pile of dirt that was part of some Desert National Wildlife Range. Nothing to write home about, that's for sure. Especially for someone like me hailing from Kentucky, with the Appalachian and Black and Sugarloaf mountains running through my home state—green with foliage, not that rocky, dirty, brown nonsense we were met with.

But there we were, baking like shake-and-bake chicken under a blazing sun, sweating to beat the band—all because that's where our Lucky Seven was found.

Kiki Cormorant. Daughter of the cousin to the mayor of Las Vegas.

Dismembered, looking like Jeff the Mannequin. Only her limbs were on the premises this time around, on account the perp was spooked, apparently.

Now, one might reasonably ask how the Feds knew they had a prostitute on their hands, given that the vic was related to the mayor and all. Thing about this serial killer was that the man surprisingly didn't do any of the hanky panky the call girls had been called for. So they were still wearing their…getup. Only missing both arms and both legs.

In Kiki's case, she showed up in full nurse regalia, wearing a uniform not from any hospital from there to Reno and LA and Phoenix. Not even from Albuquerque, which was saying something.

Now, she was dismembered behind a trash compactor, hastily stashed, by the look of it—limbs up a trail where the Bureau assumed the serial killer got away.

Sun was beating down to beat the band now, my undershirt sticking to me on our approach. Wished I'd left my bow tie back in our government-issued Burban, but it was a gift from Mama for my first day at the FBI. A regimental tie, they're called, with a solid blue background lined by red and gold strips. One of those traditional types that never goes out of style.

Dad had been the forerunner of my attire, showing how a real man dresses. But to hot Hades with that fashion-forward gesture, at least until we got out of the blazing heat!

I undid my tie and then unbuttoned the top one to my white shirt.

Kenny snorted a laugh. "That's why I go the Polo route." He grinned as he grabbed his faded, sleeveless white knit shirt, pits stained by…don't want to know what.

"And that's why you're still single, Kenny G…" I mumbled.

Gina threw a right jab into my left ribs; sometimes she had to do that.

Glad I jumped the gun on getting a bit more air. Because

on approach, hoofing it and huffing it up the trail, I nearly gagged.

Smelled like eighty pounds of ground beef that had lived well past its use-by date. Sitting in the high-noon sun. With a side of boiled cabbage.

Supposed that was the truth of it. Especially because of what awaited us.

The limbs were there, alright. Two arms, two legs. Broiling in the hundred-plus Vegas afternoon.

But where I'd expected them to be severed, maybe with a machete or chef's blade, they were something—else…

Mangled and torn, more like it!

As if some superhuman had ripped poor Kiki limb from limb. Literally.

"For the love…" Gina moaned with complaint, throwing an arm across her nose and mouth.

Good idea.

I did the same, approaching the…evidence covered with flies. Surprised coyotes hadn't yet descended, helping themselves to a leg of Kiki.

I circled the pile, that PBS special coming to mind. The four appendages were scattered about behind a group of desert bushes in a clearing along a gravel path.

"Are we sure these…limbs are Kiki's?" I asked.

Kenny G snorted. "Is there any doubt?"

I regarded the…evidence again, chipped nail polish matching the crimson lip gloss on the victim. There was also a white sleeve that matched the nurse getup. Supposed DNA would confirm it, and supposed no reason for a pile of female limbs to be chilling out along a desert path twenty miles north of the Strip.

Gina joined me now, doing her own once-over.

I asked, "Whatcha thinking, Gina colada?"

"The killer is an obvious sociopath with a complete disregard for human dignity or life."

"Obvs. But are we sure this is the same killer?"

Another snort from Kenny G. Would rather hear something along the lines of a saxophone chirp from his namesake, given we were in Vegas. But I supposed it was the Bureau, so no luck on that front.

"You kiddin' me? The MO matches to a P!"

I almost didn't know what to do with that one. To a P? Are you kidding me?

Then I LOLed, as all the kids were saying nowadays.

"What's so funny?" he asked.

"Did you really say the MO matches—to a *P?*"

He shrugged, pulling at his collar. "Yeah, so?"

"To a P? For reals?"

Now Gina joined in. And Kenny G was breathless, not at all forever in love with us pair.

He asked with a scowl, "What's your deal?"

I said, "It's to a *T*, Kenny. T. Not P."

Kenny's face fell. "Really?"

"Yuppers."

"All this time I..." And he faded off into a mumbly conversation with himself he should have had twenty years ago.

I went back to the pile, regarding the...evidence again.

"Suppose it does fit the MO—" I snickered, which rolled into a giggle "to a *T*."

Shouldn't have put the emphasis on it like I did, but it just sorta slipped.

Kenny G wasn't sentimental for our company, that's for sure, the lanky Bureau lifer sauntering away, engaged in another mumbly conversation with himself until his phone rang. He answered it while we kept at it.

"Whatcha think, Gina colada?"

She regarded the pile again. "Does seem like the same pattern. Dumped body, detached limbs. But the proximity is new."

"True that. Although, from what the report said, sounds like the perp had been spooked by some RVers on a nightly stroll."

"Then what about those tears again? Up until victim six, previous ones had their limbs severed, not ripped off like the T-Rex from Jurassic Park going at that poor scientist."

I turned to her. "Oh my cheeps, I loved that scene!"

"Can we get back to it?" Kenny G barked, ending the call.

"What's the dealio?" I ask.

Dude shoved the phone in his pocket and made a valiant effort at pressing his tarpaulin of hair back into place. Valiant, I tell ya, but no banana on that front of his manhood.

"Two more are missing."

"Prostitutes?" I asked.

"Uhh…yeah. Women."

"Of the night."

He nodded, saying nothing more.

Gina wiped her brow with a sigh. "That makes nine."

I shuddered. "*Oof.* Unlucky number nine."

"That's not a thing."

"It is for the Japanese."

"Why?"

"Because it sounds similar to their word for torture or suffering."

"Sounds about right, given the crazy we've been dealing with."

"You know…" I wiped my brow with my hand, but all I accomplished was swapping perspiration. "Could really use something to eat. Could really use—"

"Cracker Barrel!" Gina shouted, knowing me to a T (or P, in Kenny G's parlance). Well, us, given it'd been our place to powwow together. Which I knew wasn't really PC anymore these days, appropriating the customs of Native

Americans, or First Nation peoples, or whatever. But whatever. It was our place—yes, to powwow. Sure beat navelgazing around a Bureau conference table piled high with Krispy Cremes and watery slop that some assumed was coffee, with the hideous glare of fluorescent lights reflecting off the polished faux wood government-issued table.

Double *oof!*

"Care for a drive?" I asked.

She turned to me, eyes wide and mouth wider. "Yes, please!"

"Do they have one of them in these parts?"

"You mean these Western parts?"

"Well, yeah. This ain't Kenturkey," my name for my home state Kentucky. "About as many restaurants as there are churches. Which is saying something in a part of America that's still 76% percent Christian—with half of them Evangelical Protestant."

Gina said, "Churches sure are a thing in them parts."

"And it's the South, so Cracker Barrels are a thing too."

Gina had whipped out her phone, searching the nifty map app on the smartphone. Boy, was life better thanks to Steve Jobs. What'd we ever do before those little gods in our pockets?

"Apparently Vegas concurs. Whoda thunk?"

"Sweetness!" I said. "Thank you, Steve Jobarino."

"Let's saddle up, partner," Gina said, the pair of us making for our government-issued Suburban.

"Hey, where're you going?" Kenny G asked.

"Cracker Barrel," I called back without breaking pace, Gina at my side.

"You can't leave. You've got a case to work!"

"Exactly!"

And I was right. Because that's the way we rolled. Mama's Pancake Breakfast, the Cracker Barrel's Country

Boy Breakfast, and a pocket full of FBI case questions that could only find answers on full stomachs.

Thank Yeshua Almighty for the Old Country Store! And Steve Jobs for his temerity to put a Rand McNally in Gina's pocket to find one.

Gina drove; I rode shotgun. Which, given the Western state of things, sounded more fun than it really was. Hated cars, especially Suburbans, their memory burned in me being shuttled from foster family to foster family.

Much more preferred the freedom and control of a BMW motorcycle, but those aren't government-issued, at least in the States. Probably in Germany, the Bundesnachrichtendienst taking far better care of their agents than their Bureau counterparts. Too bad my ancestors had been forced to flee Bundesrepublik Deutschland, on account of a certain Führer with a flair for ovens.

Anyhoo, Dad had introduced me to the Southern comfort chain the day after I'd arrived in my new forever home. Never experienced anything like it in all my life. Not the Southern kitsch, even though Virginia had definitely been part of the Lost Cause. Never experienced the flap-jacks smothered in real syrup (no, that Aunt Jemima nonsense concocted in some backroom lab doesn't count), or bacon strips as thick as my hands, or the coffee (Dad felt if I was old enough to drive, I was old enough to drink coffee).

But that wasn't even half of it!

Kid in a candy store, I was, when Mom and Dad took me to one the first time. The Southern restaurant chain sported a gift store with a bit too much kitsch for my taste now, but back in the day it was like Disney—with all the radio controlled cars and board games, the stuffed animals and T-shirts with funny slogans. And the candy. Lots and lots of candy. Had hardly seen so much candy in all my life, on account we were never allowed to have any at the orphanage, and my foster families never sprang for it. Dad let me take as much of it home as I wanted after filling up on steak and eggs.

First thing I did when I joined the FBI and partnered with Gina was look for a Cracker Barrel. The joint had become our standard place to powwow. Solved a few cases at those tables already meeting over plates of pancakes and cheesy eggs, bacon and steak, fried apples and grits than any of our colleagues have in official Bureau discussion packed into fluorescent-lit conference rooms with burnt Folgers and Krispy Kreme donuts.

Given all the crazy, a powwow at Cracker Barrel was exactly what we needed to make sense of the case from hot Hades.

Turned out, our Cracker Barrel destination was a quick fifteen minute drive. It sat across from an EZPAWN pawn shop (killer name; obvious and to the point) and next to an In-N-Out Burger joint (why settle for fried beef when you can have all-day breakfast?).

Like the rest of Vegas, not an ounce of grass or foliage at the joint. Just dirt and rocks. A few palm trees and sick-looking bushes did offer a decent fig leaf for the Southern chain's dignity, but it wasn't much. They had the white rocking chairs, though, so at least they had that going for them.

Gina pulled in between a silver Mercedes G-Class and pink Cadillac Escalade, a Mary Kay sticker slapped to the rear window. Both felt right for the city.

Climbing out, the scent of burning wood hung heavy, along with grilled meat and something sugary. Stomach rumbled something fierce on our march across the parking lot and my head felt faint now with hunger. We took a table in the corner flanking a bay of windows and within darting distance of an emergency exit.

Because if I'd learned anything while at the FBI, it was

to be within eyeshot of an emergency exit. Never knew when the shiznit would hit the fan, and a quick escape you would need.

Our waitress, a mellow teeny bopper named Ariel (with red hair and green pants, too; no kidding) looked like she could use the all-day breakfast option herself. She took our orders pronto.

Tea and Mama's Pancake Breakfast for Gina, complete with three buttermilk pancakes, scrambled eggs, and thickly slicked bacon. The Cracker Barrel's Country Boy Breakfast was always up my alley, with a sirloin steak I had to cajole into getting moo-ready rare on top of three eggs sunny-side up along with fried apples, hash brown casserole, grits, and biscuits and gravy, along with the best cup of Joe this side of the Mississippi—well, the other side, since it was imported into the West.

Figured I'd earned it after the morning we'd had.

The food fit the decor, a collection of Americana kitsch that bespoke a good-'ol-days era that never really existed. A bright red metal Coca-Cola sign with signs of rusted age hung on a wall above our table, surrounded by black-and-white framed pictures of the Dust Bowl era. No roaring fire though, which sorta made sense given the temps were pushing the low 100s, but I was disappointed anyway. The woodsmoke I'd smelled must have come from their grills. At least a buck with a large rack was anchored above the mantle, along with a flintlock rifle underneath.

Soon, Ariel was back with water and hot beverages. I leaned back and threw back a swig of the brew. Heaven. A light roast that was balanced, sweet, and full of caramelly flavor without all the hippie caramel flavor nonsense peeps add to Joe these days.

Finishing my swig, I grabbed the triangle peg game I loved as a child. I'd whip Dad every time.

Gina had dragged along an accordion file stuffed with

case goodies. Autopsies, eye witness accounts, what scant evidence had been left behind. She spread some of it out.

I kept at the peg game. Was a way for me to clear my head and give my fingers something to do. My fingers needed that when the pressure ratcheted and anxiety threatened to bloom into overwhelm. Usually my thumbing tick worked, but I was over it. Needed something else, and the pegs were it.

"Remember this one?"

She held up a set of photographs showing dark, wet concrete overexposed by the flash—with Jeff the Mannequin's mistress in a She-Ra costume. Kid you not. The white leotard, accented by gold polygon planted on her buxom chest, flaring gold shoulder pads. Imagined she'd be sporting gold wristbands and complementary gold boots. Maybe even sporting the Sword of Protection, complete with the glowing jewel in the hilt that allowed Princess Adora to channel her powers.

But no banana on that front, given her limbs were missing, and blood was still freshly oozing by the time we arrived.

Shoving the peg game away, I snorted a laugh. "How could I forget?"

Unlucky number six. Broad was found lying face-first just inside the lip to what was affectionately called The Tunnel—a massive, well, tunnel running under all that glitzes and glisters on the Strip. It was basically a storm drain meant to protect the city from flash floods. Come to find out, an entire population of mole people lived in The Tunnel, burrowed under the city.

One of said mole peeps found the woman after being startled awake. Dude was three sheets to the wind by the time we took his testimony, combined with a strong grassy smell emanating from the man. I might be ethnically Jewish, and religiously Christian, but I knew wacky tobacky when I saw it—or smelled it, as was the case at the sixth victim's crime scene.

So, taking into consideration those twin elements to the witness, we weren't banking on much. Testimony was sure something to noodle on, though.

Mole Man swore he saw some hulking figure over her. Eight feet tall, huffing and puffing, throwing up a roary, snorty, skittering screech that made Mole Man crap his pants. Literally, too, because we could smell it.

Lucky for his manly dignity, the ganga he'd been smoking in those tunnels covered most of the stench. Which made us super skeptical of his story of things. Especially the part about the She-Ra's counterpart He-Man tearing her limbs off with his bare hands and looking like the infamous Lizard Man of Scape Ore Swamp, all scaley and slimy, smelling of a rotting tank.

Didn't stay around long enough to dive deeper into it all. Gina had tossed her cheese and I nearly joined her. Wasn't even from coming face to face with limbless She-Ra either (which we later learned was part of an escort service's superhero shtick). It was the ungodly, rank smell of the joint. Took me back to my days of soiled beds and mold-streaked walls—the orphanage not giving one hot damn whether half a dozen of the kiddos pissed or crapped their bed during the night or the roof was leaking and flaring up mold spores in the walls.

And there we were, standing in the middle of a long, dark tunnel that stank to high heaven like a basement filled with diaper pales.

So we bolted after Mole Man's...*testimony*. If you could call it that.

Funny thing was, though when we seized footage from a Sunoco on the topside of the Tunnel storm drain, it did bolster the credibility of the wits testimony—some. Still had that ganga to contend with, but a bulky man, hairy and...

well, sorta scaly looking did come scampering out at dawn. So that certainly took both the cheesecake and red velvet cake—since it gave us a solid lead and was weirder than words.

Didn't know what to make of it, not in the slightest, but it did start to clue us into the fact this serial killer case was not as it seemed.

Gina set the photos down in front of me and rifled through the others. Vics One through Five. Seven we were already acquainted with, but…it was all just a jumbled jigsaw that would give Ravensburger and Buffalo Games puzzle companies a run for their money.

"So what's our ellie?" I asked with a sigh, throwing back a swig of brew. Just on the edge of going bad; not yet too lukewarm, but getting there. Had a certain tolerance for my coffee temp, my mouth super sensitive and intolerant to anything below a hundo Fahrenheit.

"Good question. The L to the E is always the golden goose."

"Sort of mixing metaphors there, aren't you, Gina colada?"

"*Psht.* Whatev. As far as I'm concerned, the likely explanation has got to be some local loner. Probably middle-age, with mommy issues. Never married, probably never had a girlfriend. Maybe never felt comfortable around women."

"So a gay?"

She frowned. "First, it's not *a* gay. Second, you can't say that these days."

I reddened, realizing my tongue-slip. Then I took a breath and shook it away.

Recovering, I asked, "So, what, he's scared of women?"

"Not sure scared is the right way to frame it. *Hates*, more like it."

"Women generally, or prostitutes specifically?"

She leaned back, staring at the ceiling. "Good question. Not there yet."

I joined her, reclining and looking at the exposed ceiling of industrial roofing material painted black. Was supposed to give it a rustic look, but it just looked janky. Didn't mind in the slightest, because the pancakes more than made up for the decor.

We both sat noodling, when a feeling came over me. Something about the case that had struck me from the beginning, combined with one of the eyewitnesses and compounded by a fresh breath filling my lungs, a warmness skating across my skin, a revelation bubbling up to the surface.

That happened sometimes in these cases, what I would call a supernatural…impression, like a shining (per Stephen King) from the Holy Spirit, guiding me along. Not as charismatic as Gina—her having been raised in the charismatic Catholic tradition; me having been born an ethnic Jew only to find Jesus as my Messiah in a Baptist foster family (only in America!)—but I'd come around to the direct influence of the Third Person of the Trinity over the years in my study of the Unseen Realm.

Both the good, holy side of it, and the not-so-good, wicked side of it.

Now was one of those times something was coming into a hearing.

"Earth to Eli…" Gina said, tapping a hand on the table that rattled the flatware. I sat forward; she asked, "Whatcha got for me?"

"I don't know. Something about what the one witness saw. The hulking figure with superhuman strength, scurrying around and smelling like the reptile exhibit at the DC zoo."

"Wasn't that the guy who was stoned out of his mind?"

"No, that was the other witness. This was the gas station

attendant who saw the scuffle and recognized the man from earlier."

"Tisha Wainwright."

"Bingo."

"What about it?"

I swallowed, gathering my thoughts. "Well, what if what she saw was a demon?"

"A demon?" Gina exclaimed, eliciting some stares from next door.

She frowned and leaned in closer, whispering again: "A demon?"

"A demon."

"As in a demon demon?"

"Is there an echo in here?" I muttered. "Well, maybe not a demon, per se. But someone possessed by one."

"Suppose someone dismembering prostitutes has to be possessed by something. What made you think of this ellie?"

"The L to the E smacks of Scripture?"

"The Bible is the likely explanation?"

"A story from the Gospel of Mark. Here, let me…"

Always carried a pocket New Testament Bible in my back pocket. Couldn't help it. Was as natural to me as some of the agents who carried a flask in their breast pocket. Yeah, they didn't know I knew; I knew.

I pulled it out and flipped to Mark 5. I ran my finger down the pages, then read:

They came to the other side of the sea, to the country of the Gerasenes. And when he had stepped out of the boat, immediately a man out of the tombs with an unclean spirit met him. He lived among the tombs; and no one could restrain him any more, even with a chain; for he had often been restrained with shackles and chains, but the chains he wrenched apart, and the shackles he broke in pieces; and no one had the strength to subdue him. Night and day among the tombs and on the mountains he was always howling and bruising himself with stones.

When he saw Jesus from a distance, he ran and bowed down before him; and he shouted at the top of his voice, "What have you to do with me, Jesus, Son of the Most High God? I adjure you by God, do not torment me." For he had said to him, "Come out of the man, you unclean spirit!" Then Jesus asked him, "What is your name?" He replied, "My name is Legion; for we are many." He begged him earnestly not to send them out of the country.

Now there on the hillside a great herd of swine was feeding; and the unclean spirits begged him, "Send us into the swine; let us enter them." So he gave them permission. And the unclean spirits came out and entered the swine; and the herd, numbering about two thousand, rushed down the steep bank into the sea, and were drowned in the sea.

The swineherds ran off and told it in the city and in the country. Then people came to see what it was that had happened. They came to Jesus and saw the demoniac sitting there, clothed and in his right mind, the very man who had had the legion; and they were afraid. Those who had seen what had happened to the demoniac and to the swine reported it. Then they began to beg Jesus to leave their neighborhood.

As he was getting into the boat, the man who had been possessed by demons begged him that he might be with him. But Jesus refused, and said to him, "Go home to your friends, and tell them how much the Lord has done for you, and what mercy he has shown you." And he went away and began to proclaim in the Decapolis how much Jesus had done for him; and everyone was amazed.

· · ·

Food finally came as I finished up reading, dishes piled with sweet-smelling flapjacks, as we called 'em in Kenturkey, and savory cheesy eggs, and salt bacon and grits. A feast fit for a king! Or at least two very hungry FBI agents. Our waitress even brought me a fresh mug of Joe, bless her heart!

A dove for the cheesy eggs first, shoving a forkful in my mouth to explain further.

When my phone buzzed.

Chewing, I pulled it out and answered it.

"Fox."

"It's Kenny."

"We're eating."

"So what, I've got news."

"Nope. We're eating. At Cracker Barrel, no less. Never interrupt the—"

"Who is it?" Gina asked.

"Kenny G."

"Don't call me that," the agent bellowed.

She giggled. "Put it on speaker, would you?"

I almost protested, but relented. No one disturbed my Cracker Barrel time, but I supposed we were on the clock.

So I punched it to speaker.

"Shoot Kenny."

Gina threw me a raised brow. "Is that a command, or do you got a comma in there somewhere, pal?"

"Fine. Shoot—" long pause "—Kenny."

"There you go." She addressed the phone. "You got a lead?"

"Sure do!" Kenny G answered. "Picked up our perp on CCTV footage from the RV park."

I crunched into my bacon. Salty Nirvana…

"And…?"

"And…you've got footage to connect with hours of Vegas CCTV footage to compare to track down our perp."

"Joy…"

"Thanks, Kenny," Gina said. "We'll finish up here and head over."

Kenny signed off, and we got back to our meal.

Ate in silence for a while before Gina asked, "By the way, what's the deal with The Cheesecake Factory, anyhow?"

I sat back, polishing off my bacon and averting my eyes, casting them about the joint; I did that sometimes.

My eye avoidance wasn't as bad as some autistic people I knew. Not that there was anything wrong with it. To each their own and all that jazz. For me, it was when the anxiety ratcheted up. Usually from embarrassment, like if I didn't understand something or I couldn't figure something out, and quite often when I didn't get a joke or a punny expression.

Then there were the times I just flat didn't want to engage. Because it was too personal, too painful, too soul-ish. Had been burned too much to let that happen again.

But…

I took a breath, then a beat. Figured I should step out on a limb with my newish partner, open up a bit. Didn't want to; not in the slightest. Just knew I should.

But I didn't have to like it.

"Nevermind," Gina said, waving a dismissive bacon slice.

"No, it's fine," I said.

"Seriously, I shouldn't have—"

"If you must know…" I began with interruption, trying to open up to my new partner, who I imagined I'd be spending oodles of time with in the bowels of the Hoover Building. "The orphanage I was at for a tenth of my life before being shipped off to my first of eleven foster families—"

"Wait, first of *eleven*?"

"Is there an echo in here? Yes, the first of eleven foster families."

"For the love…"

"Nope. It wasn't for love, I can tell you that much. The Commonwealth of Virginia pays up to two G per child and six-to-seven hundo per month. So it literally pays to foster."

Gina went silent, staring down at the Mama's Pancake Breakfast she'd polished off.

"So, The Cheesecake Factory…" I started.

She glanced up with a shrug. "What's the deal with that, anyway?"

"Like I was saying, the orphanage I was at for a tenth of my life before being shipped off to my first of eleven foster families would take the orphans to a local franchise of the national chain for Christmas every year."

Gina hummed and shifted straighter. "That doesn't seem so bad. A trip into suburbia for a special meal."

"Ahh, but that's where you missed it, Gina colada."

She giggled at that, the little nickname I called her, sounding like her favorite Caribbean pineapple and coconut adult-rum beverage.

"What did I miss?"

"The part where I said the orphanage took the orphans to a local franchise of the national chain for Christmas every year."

"You were an orphan, silly-pants."

"I was…but not *the orphans*."

Furrowing her brow she took a sip of tea and took that in, looking over my shoulder with contemplation.

Took her a bit, then a beat. Then she had it.

"For the love…you weren't one of the orphans, were you?"

"Bingo."

She set her tea down now, nostrils flaring and face reddening with heat.

"They left you behind?" she said with indignation. Then added: "On Christmas?"

The word echoed around the joint with a bit too much flair, eliciting a few furrowed stairs from the surrounding tables. But I appreciated the gesture just the same.

I grabbed my brew and took a sip. Then promptly grimaced.

Lukewarm!

Blech!

I frowned and set it down, responding with a simple, "Bingo."

"Suppose I can understand why you hate the place."

Then she smiled, sitting straighter. As if something dawned on her.

"And why everything bad takes the *cheese*cake."

I grinned. "Double bingo."

Downing the rest of her tea, she stood. "Come on, partner. We've got some footage to review."

I did not down my beverage, but joined her, the pair of us walking out with a bit more understanding.

Sure wasn't used to it, being understood. Much more evasive about the personal baggage. And yet…

Kinda liked it. Being understood.

Soon, we were at the local FBI Field Office, Kenny G's own government-issued vehicle (a black Ford Taurus; Uncle Sam doesn't discriminate against domestic car manufacturers) anchored in the visitor's spot. Figured.

Gina parked next to him (because technically we were visiting, from Washington), and we made our way inside a nondescript, black and glass two-story building that screamed Feds.

Waiting for us inside was Kenny G, who led us back into a tiny room with a bay of monitors. Spreading his arms out, he said, "Footage."

I looked at him and frowned. Not my idea of gumshoeing it, but alright.

Gina and I each took a seat and then spent the next two hours that way. Just propped up in our chairs in front of a bay of monitors, black and white video footage from who knew how many cameras filtering across my face.

From casinos and restaurants. Along the Strip and elsewhere around on Vegas streets. People gambling. People eating. People checking in and checking out, coming in and out of bedrooms.

Four hours later, we came up empty.

"Bupkis!" I complained, leaning back and rubbing my eyes.

"Same here," Gina echoed with complaint, throwing up a cat yawn and going to her feet. She started pacing, rubbing her temples. Wanted to join her, but more than anything I wanted to solve this case that had stumped LVMPD and my FBI colleagues.

Because if I could be the one to bring that gigolo joker to justice—well, I'd have it made! No more Spooky Eli or Doc Doolittle, that's for sure. The boys back at the Farm would have to respect the man who brought a nine-time serial killer down. Wouldn't be Ted Bundy or John Wayne Gacy level, the sicko psychos murdering some thirty people a piece. But look at all the accolades John Keenan got when he brought down the Son of Sam, and David Berkowitz had only killed seven women.

Mine had killed nine! Severed their limbs, for goodness' sake. Or ripped them off, if Mole Man was to be believed.

But, first things first…

I stood and stretched my back, sauntering to a cart with a coffee carafe and set of chipped government-issued, white mugs. Not even an FBI log, just sad-looking Walmart specials. But, beggars can't be choosers. So I snatched one and pumped some brew. Steam rose as the black liquid squirted into the mug, the smell of cardboard and dirt rising on a hot breath.

I winced, then chanced a sip. And grimaced.

Blech!

Cardboard and dirt is right. Snatching a sugar packet (which was a big, fat negatory in my coffee connoisseur book!), I tore it and dumped it. Same for a can of powdered creamer (a second big, fat negatory in my coffee connoisseur book!) and dumped a mound of it on top the black brew.

The ant-hill clump settled down to the bottom, joining the sugar. I stirred the concoction together, the black sludge spinning into a mesmerizing swirl of off-white until it all turned the color of brown-sugared oat meal. Not a good look for a cup of Joe worth its salt.

But desperate times called for desperate measures. So I threw back a swig, bracing for an assault on my tastebuds.

I shrugged. Not half bad.

Gina leaned over. "Any tea on that cart?"

"Nope. Sorry."

"For the love…"

I settled back into my chair. "Catch anything on your end?"

"Nothing but nothing."

"About the long and short of it on my end, too."

Another swig, bracing for another assault. Again, not bad.

Which made me feel like there was something wrong with me! Never had I never used cream and sugar in coffee. Dad taught me well.

But threw back another, then drained half of it and set it aside. Would need the caffeine for the rest of the afternoon.

Rest of the afternoon was right! The pair of us got back on the pony and scrolled through another pile of DVDs burned with days of footage, the viewer set to double speed to lend a helping hand.

Thought my eyeballs would pop out of my sockets, it was so mind-numbingly—

Now hold on…

Something caught my eye. Some random camera in—what's that? A cemetery?

"That's strange…" I muttered, winding back the footage.

"Whatcha got?" Gina asked, sauntering over with another yawn.

"Don't know, but…check this out."

"Sure thing, chicken wing."

She slid next to me. I pointed at the monitor showing a ramshackle structure of boxes and sheets against the backside of a large statue in Woodlawn Cemetery on the north side of Vegas. The Virgin Mary herself, by the look of it.

Couldn't be sure but…something caught my eye. Something familiar.

Very familiar.

Gina squinted, leaning forward. Then gasped.

"Is that—"

"A hand and a foot? Yuppers. Looks that way to me."

"Egads!" She sat back and folded her arms. "Which means…"

"An arm and a leg ain't too far away."

Pokin' out from the tent structure thingy was indeed a hand and foot. White, with painted nails. Couldn't make out the color in the grayscale, but I imagined they were hot pink or sky blue or emerald green, maybe tangerine orange or plumb purple, or candy apple red to match Kiki Comorant's nurse getup—just like all the other victims.

Gina startled. "What's that?"

Good question.

A hulking man was now sauntering down the road.

Gigantic, imposing. Shoulders broad like an ox. Wore tattered pants but was shirtless, and very hairy and—were those scales? Skin sure looked like it was puckered and wrinkled, like a wax figure had a run in with a blowtorch. Looked like a cross between the Hulk Hogan and Harry from *Harry and the Hendersons* (a fave movie from one of my foster families), and Lizard Man of Scape Ore Swamp. One of the more gentle varieties of all three…but still!

Sent shivers ratcheting up my spine and blooming in my limbs. Like the sight of the—*being* had made me fear losing them.

The—man, I guess, made for the tent, then slipped inside. When he did, we glimpsed even more familiar somethings.

I jumped back. "Sweet mother of Melchizedek!"

"For the love!" Gina shouted.

"That's what I said!"

Gina was heaving breaths, hand covering her mouth. "Is that what I think it is?"

Couldn't answer. Didn't need to, but the words wouldn't come. Thought I was gonna lose my Cracker Barrel, then and there!

Because…yeah, it was exactly what she thought it was.

Limbs stacked like a cord of firewood, one on top the other. By my count, at least a dozen, maybe two. Which would make sense. It was simple math.

Two times two equaled four.

Four times six equaled twenty-four.

As in, the six missing vics—minus Lucky Seven, whose arms and legs were baking in the Vegas sun up a trail in an RV park north of town. London-broil style.

"Where is this?" Gina had her phone out with map app at the ready.

"Woodland Cemetery, in North Vegas."

She started doing her iPhone thing—when something hit me.

"Oh my cheeps…"

"What?" Gina bolted to the bank of monitors.

"No, not the footage. Mark 5!"

"As in, the Gospel?"

"Bingo." I swallowed, then quoted, "'*This man lived in the tombs, and no one could bind him anymore, not even with a chain. For he had often been chained hand and foot, but he tore the chains apart and broke the irons on his feet. No one was strong enough to subdue him.*'"

"The psycho's living in a cemetery…" Gina marveled.

"Much like the Gerasene Demoniac."

"With pieces of his victims!"

"Prizes, no doubt."

"Got that right," she said. "But what about that last bit?"

"What bit?" I asked.

"The part about no one being strong enough to subdue him?"

That gave me pause.

"We'll have to be ready," she went on. "Full tactical team and all."

"Guns ablazing?"

"This ain't the Wild West."

I chuckled and spread my arms around the joint. "Look around, sister. Where are we?"

"We're in the West. Vegas West. With the Strip and Bellagio Fountain and The Cheesecake Factory! Just not the Wild West."

"Touché. Fine, not blazing. Guns at the ready, then."

Gina stood. "We better tell Kenny and get a team over there, stat."

Tried to protest, but she was already out the door after the agent.

I sat and stewed. Tell Kenny G? It was my find—*our* find, I corrected myself. Gina and me. Besides, no way was a government-issued suit from the Wild West gonna believe some homeless dude living in a cemetery north of the Strip was possessed—by a minion of the Devil himself.

And I was right. The Ken-meister didn't believe a word of it. Definitely not Mark 5 and barely the CCTV footage. It was only after we pieced together some more, retracing the man's steps, connecting it back to the RV park, that he realized we were right and he was wrong.

Didn't push on that one. Could easily have rubbed it in his face but didn't. A first for me, always wanting to take the credit, take the glory, but I let it go.

See, I could be taught. Sometimes.

But to Kenny G's credit, he did rally the troops and off we went. Two tactical teams and a brigade of LVMPD's finest. A bit overkill in my book. Then again, we did have a serial killer on our hands, outpacing even David Berkowitz. And it seemed like we had a demon possessed one at that, recapitulating one kind of possession from the Gospels themselves. Not very creative on the part of the Unseen Realm, sort of a dead giveaway.

Then again, not sure I would have ever thought of demons as the creative sort. After all, their MO was more about demolition and destruction than creation and construction.

So, off we went, racing to Woodlawn in our Suburban behind full-armored tactical vehicles left over from Operation Enduring Freedom. Uncle Sam needed to offload the leftovers from Bush's war somewhere, and police forces around the country were more than willing to take them off 43's hands. Swapped the desert camo for urban black, but they looked just as menacing.

In no time flat, we were rounding the entrance into the modest cemetery, a sad sort of affair, even for a cemetery.

Took up all of half a block, sandwiched between an indus-trial park and a middle-class neighborhood that had seen better days, with rusted chain link fences and cracked plastic baby swings joining smashed glass Bud bottles and crunched Miller cans strewn about.

The cemetery itself didn't look much better, needing a visit from TruGreen lawn care and Hydro-Rain sprinklers. Twigs posing as trees with a bit of lichen on top, like the model railroad variety Dad and me planted all over my train set, rested on their laurels while the dead lay in repose.

But we came in screaming like bats out of hell. Supposed it was warranted, given the demon from hell that was planted behind a statue of the Virgin Mary.

Kenny G was in the lead tactical van (of course!), while Gina and me trailed at the back. The caravan split once we reached the encampment, surrounding the dilapidated structure of sun-kissed cardboard and moldy sheets on all sides.

"Here we go…" I said, throwing open the door and lunging out, Glock drawn.

Had never done that before. Was much more a desk jockey than anything resembling CBS's *Criminal Minds*. Always a first.

Same for Gina, who didn't even have her Glock drawn.

"What's the dealio?" I asked, raising my weapon and nodding toward it.

"Uh, forgot it," she said.

Didn't get a retort in, as Kenny G and his g-men jumped out and got to it. Doors thrown open and guns (big guns; assault rifle big) aimed at the ramshackle encampment. The lead agent sported government-issued shades along with his Glock.

Nothing but crickets from inside. No movement, no noises. Nada.

Even the wind seemed to take a breath from all the commotion.

We held our position, waiting for word on what was next.

Kenny gave it, coming out from behind his Suburban and inching toward the shelter. Dude with a death wish, he was!

"This is the FBI," he commanded. "We have you surrounded. Come out with your hands—"

Before I knew it, Kenny G was on his back, those last words still lodged in his throat—sunglasses and Glock sailing through the air.

With the Vegas psycho on top at his throat—throwing up a horrifying roary, snorty, skittering screech!

"Hold your fire," one of the lead g-men commanded, all of us pivoting our weapons toward the scene with tightening grip but holding fast.

Good call. Didn't know what to do about it. Not in the slightest. Was too caught off-guard by the sight of the burly man, shirtless and hairy (like Harry from childhoods past!) to do anything about it.

Then…

Then Mark 5 came rushing to the surface at the sight: *'This man lived in the tombs, and no one could bind him anymore, not even with a chain. For he had often been chained hand and foot, but he tore the chains apart and broke the irons on his feet. No one was strong enough to subdue him.'*

No one could subdue was right!

Was like something out of a Stephen King fever dream! Cujo, this was, the monstrous Saint Bernard who terrorized that small town of Castle Rock, Maine. Fake town, but terrorized!

Like that, this was that!

Someone shouted from Kenny's vehicle, "Take the shot if you've got it!"

The pair flipped over, with Kenny now on top and the psycho on the bottom. The agent's face was bluer than the government-issued fluorescent shades he'd had just moments ago.

"No, no! Hold your fire!" someone else shouted from another SUV.

There was a sudden roary, snorty, skittering screech again. From the psycho, a hot breath gusting our way—whether from the beastish man or the Vegas desert, it wasn't clear. Then there was the stench of it all. Rotten eggs and reptilian tang.

Then psycho man flipped Kenny back on his back.

And everyone tightened their grips and jostled forward, closing in on the pair still going at it on the dry grass.

"Hold your fire!" someone shouted, but we were all itching for the shot to end it all.

There was pandemonium. No one knew what to do.

Gina inched behind me, throwing up a squeal. "What do we do?"

"I don't know." And I didn't. Was never in that sort of position before.

Sweat ran down my face in the 90-degree heat, the sun sinking fast now and darkness encroaching on the wicked darkness that had already enveloped the team.

"Just pray…" Gina finally squeaked.

"Good idea."

So that's what I did.

Not sure why, looking back, but there was a prayer lodged way back in my lizard brain—the one reared in the Christian faith and fueled by the Mark 5 recognition.

Holstering my gun, I reached inside my shirt, squeezing my hand slick with sweat down past my Kevlar vest, and yanked out a golden cross I'd gotten in Rome on a family trip.

Something seemed to instantly shift in the melee at the center, the psycho jolting with a shudder—

And glancing my way!

So I thrust out the article of faith and got to it, praying: "Jesus Christ rebuke you, O Satan!"

The beastish man flailed at the mention of Jesus's name.

Then I added my prayer, pleading with the Holy Trinity for assistance: "Oh God, come to my assistance! Oh Lord, make haste to help me! Oh Everlasting God, who have ordained and created the ministries of angels and men in wonderful order: Mercifully grant that, as your holy angels serve you in heaven, they may help and defend us on earth at your command. Through our Lord Jesus Christ, your son, who lives and reigns with you in the unity of the Holy Spirit, one God, forever and ever. Amen."

A cackle broke out from the beast, spinning into hysterical giggling, almost like a spoiled child. Soon, his body started heaving with guffawing belly laughs from deep inside.

But it was the window the rest of the men needed to jump the man, wrestling him off from Kenny G and down to the ground.

Took five burly officers to finally bring the perp under control, but they managed to shackle his wrists with cuffs, joined by several yards of heavy chains.

Apparently, Kenny's g-men weren't taking any chances.

Until…

Another roary, snorty, skittering screech erupted from the man. He arched his back, strained against the cords of chains, and busted through them.

One.

By.

One.

Until he was free!

More pandemonium, more confusion at what to do.

I thrust my cross back out and prayed again:

"Almighty and eternal God, who appointed your only-begotten Son the Redeemer of the world, and willed to be appeased by his blood: Grant, we beseech you, that we may so honor this, the price of our redemption, and by its virtue be so defended from the evils of our present life, so as to enjoy its fruit in heaven forevermore, through the name of Jesus Christ Our Lord. Amen."

The beastish man stumbled again at the sound of Jesus' name, the prayer seeming to lull the demon within this man.

Which was all the boys in black needed.

A *one-two-three* punch from someone aiming from stage right sent the man falling to his knees.

He arched his back, screaming again, until another *pop-pop-pop* ended it all—the man slumping to his face and going still.

I lowered my arm, Gina came up to my side.

It was over.

"Nice shot," she said to a burly man coming in with raised weapon. A rifle. "Too bad he met his Maker. Would've been nice for him to pay for his crimes."

"Don't worry, he will."

Before I turned to him, the others rushing to the perp and securing him with cords of galvanized steel cables now to bring him under control, I glanced at the body—then saw it.

"Tranquilizers."

The man nodded. "That's right. He'll pay. Mark my words. The bastard will pay."

I smiled. "Sweetness. And Gina was right. Nice shot."

The man nodded and sauntered off to help bag his catch.

As they hoisted the man to an awaiting transport van, Kenny shuffled our way, battered and bruised and heaving stabilizing breaths—but he was alive. Had lived to tell a tale his grand children some day would be spreading far and wide for years.

"That man—" he took a breath, then added: "that beast…it was like he was possessed or something!"

"That's because he was," I said, matter-of-factly.

He turned to me, mouth open as if in a question, eyes wide and chest heaving. Didn't know whether he was readying to laugh in my face or if I'd confirmed his deepest, darkest, most horrifying suspicions.

Didn't say a word. Just blinked, then again. "Thanks, Elijah. For everything. You did good, kid. Real good."

Then he sauntered away, saying nothing more.

"You were right," Gina said. "Just like this man in Mark's Gospel."

I shook my head, disbelieving it all. "Too weird for words."

"And scary…"

I nodded. "And that."

We stood there, watching the van peel away in a cloud of Vegas dust, the suspect safe and secure.

For now…

"Can hardly believe it myself," Gina said. "Sure it all wasn't the result of illicit drug use, infusing him with the abilities, cocaine or ecstasy?"

I shook my head. "Nope. Doubt they'll find any of that in his bloodstream."

"Then what?"

I shrugged. "What else but demonic possession?"

"You think? I find that hard to believe."

"Why?"

"It's not that I don't believe in demons. The Bible sure indicates they're real, and my charismatic Catholic upbringing certainly primed me for their possibility."

"But…"

Gina smirked. "Butts are for toilets."

I furrowed my brow at the funny expression. "Uh, well, yeah. Suppose so. Still: But…"

"But…well, because it's so unbelievable!"

"What is, that the Unseen Realm is breaking into our seen one?"

"Well, yeah! Not an everyday thing, you know?"

I shrugged. "Unless it happens far more often, but we're not aware of it."

She opened her mouth for a reply, but snapped it shut. "Maybe…"

"Don't have it all worked out myself. Either way, just glad we got the bastard."

"Word."

We stood there for a few beats as the van drove off.

I finally broke the silence: "The man who—" I turned to Gina "*almost* got away."

"Would have, too," she answered, "had it not been for your Holy Spirit insight."

"Suppose so."

"What do you think it means?"

I turned to Gina. "What do you mean?"

She gestured toward the cloud still riding high from LVMPD tires kicking up the Vegas dirt and grim, heat waves obscuring the view but still a sight to behold, the guy we'd nabbed being carted away—justice served, and all that.

"That man had been possessed. By a demon!" Sounded like she'd come around after all.

"Right…"

"Something not of this world had set up shop in our world and—"

Gina took a beat, then a breath, wiping her brow dripping with sweat. I did the same, wondering what she was getting at.

"It's just…" she went on, "I grew up Catholic. A charismatic Catholic at that."

"Right…"

"So this sort of thing is in our wheelhouse. Believing in demons, even their presence and activity in our world."

I snorted a laugh. "Well, not my wheelhouse! After all, Baptists aren't too keen on seeing demons behind every car accident or pandemic. Maybe the latest presidential election or Supreme Court case that doesn't go their way."

"I'm serious!"

"Me too!"

Gina huffed and folded her arms, the pair of us still gazing at the contrail of road dust from LVMPD's finest.

"What I mean is, this takes the cake."

"You mean cheesecake. Because you know how much I hate that stuff."

"Right. Cheesecake. What went down, what we witnessed…"

Now she turned to me, looking me dead in the eyes and not breaking. Which sort of creeped me out. Wasn't that into eye contact. More into facial avoidance, especially for prolonged periods of time. But…she held me.

"What does it mean, Eli?"

I shrugged. "It means what it is."

"What's that supposed to mean?"

"What I said. Or rather, what you said."

"And what was that?"

"The man was possessed by a demon."

She huffed again, something she was doing a lot of lately. "And what does that mean?"

"It means…"

I trailed off, not really knowing what it meant, actually. What *did* it mean?

I wasn't sure. What I was sure of was that something had changed, something had shifted in our reality. Or at least my own, my awareness of what had probably been there all along but was too ignorant—willfully or not, wasn't yet sure—to see it, to believe it.

What I *was* sure of, was that the Unseen Realm was real, it was not silent, and it was roaming across Earth—seeking to devour anyone who stood in its way.

And prostitute or not, I wouldn't let that happen again. Not on my watch, not on my life.

"All I can say is, what I saw," I finally said, adding, "what *we* saw—the Unseen Realm broke into our seen one. Now, what that means? For us, for the Bureau—for our country, the world? I can't say exactly. But it does seem like a development."

Gina smirked. "I'd say."

A thought crossed my mind, and I smiled. "Maybe we'll join forces one day to investigate these x-files of the Church. Wouldn't that be rad?"

She laughed, then smiled. "I'd like that. The pair of us standing against the darkness."

I nodded, liking the sound of that. "Standing against the darkness, indeed."

Silence fell between us as the dust cloud began to dissipate down the way, the LVMPD van having disappeared now.

We'd done it, Gina and I. We'd solved a case straight from hot Hades.

No. Straight from the Unseen Realm.

Just hoped what happened in Vegas stayed in Vegas.

What it would mean for me, for both of us—Gina and me—and our department at the Bureau…Well, Yeshua Almighty only knew.

Which was enough to call it a day.

ENJOY LUCK BE THE LADIES?

A big thanks for joining Elijah Fox and Gina Anderson on their investigation saving the world! **Here's what's next:**

Want to join Elijah Fox and Gina Anderson solving more supernatural mysteries? Dive into solving more Group X cases:
www.groupxcases.com.

If you loved the book and have a moment to spare, **a short review is much appreciated**. Nothing fancy, just your honest take. Spreading the word is probably the #1 way you can help independent authors like me and help others enjoy the story.

GET YOUR FREE THRILLER

Building a relationship with my readers is one of my all-time favorite joys of writing! Once in a while I like to send out a newsletter with giveaways, free stories, pre-release content, updates on new books, and other bits on my stories.

Join my insider's group for updates, giveaways, and your free novel—a full-length action-adventure story in my *Order of Thaddeus* thriller series. Just tell me where to send it.

Follow this link to subscribe:
www.jabouma.com/free

ALSO BY J. A. BOUMA

Nobody should have to read bad religious fiction—whether it's cheesy plots with pat answers or misrepresentations of the Christian faith and the Bible. So J. A. Bouma tells compelling, propulsive stories that thrill as much as inspire, offering a dose of insight along the way.

Order of Thaddeus Action-Adventure Thriller Series

Holy Shroud • Book 1

The Thirteenth Apostle • Book 2

Hidden Covenant • Book 3

American God • Book 4

Grail of Power • Book 5

Templars Rising • Book 6

Rite of Darkness • Book 7

Gospel Zero • Book 8

The Emperor's Code • Book 9

Deadly Hope • Book 10

Fallen Ones • Book 11

Silas Grey Collection 1 (Books 1-3)

Silas Grey Collection 2 (Books 4-6)

Silas Grey Collection 3 (Books 7-9)

Backstories: Short Story Collection 1

Martyrs Bones: Short Story Collection 2

Group X Cases Supernatural Suspense Series

Not of This World • Book 1

The Darkest Valley • Book 2

Luck Be the Ladies (Novelette)

Ichthus Chronicles Sci-Fi Apocalyptic Series

Apostasy Rising / Season 1, Episode 1

Apostasy Rising / Season 1, Episode 2

Apostasy Rising / Season 1, Episode 3

Apostasy Rising / Season 1, Episode 4

Apostasy Rising / Full Season 1 (Episodes 1 to 4)

Apocalypse Rising / Season 2, Episode 1

Apocalypse Rising / Season 2, Episode 2

Apocalypse Rising / Season 2, Episode 3

Apocalypse Rising / Season 2, Episode 4

Apocalypse Rising / Full Season 2 (Episodes 1 to 4)

Faith Reimagined Spiritual Coming-of-Age Series

A Reimagined Faith • Book 1

A Rediscovered Faith • Book 2

Mill Creek Junction Short Story Series

The New Normal • Collection 1

My Name's Johnny Pope • Collection 2

Joy to the Junction! • Collection 3

The Ties that Bind Us • Collection 4

A Matter of Justice • Collection 5

Get all the latest short stories at: www.millcreekjunction.com

Find all of my latest book releases at: www.jabouma.com

ABOUT THE AUTHOR

J. A. Bouma believes nobody should have to read bad religious fiction—whether it's cheesy plots with pat answers or misrepresentations of the Christian faith and the Bible. So he tells compelling, propulsive stories that thrill as much as inspire, while offering a dose of insight along the way.

As a former congressional staffer and pastor, and award-nominated bestselling author of over forty religious fiction and nonfiction books, he blends a love for ideas and adventure, exploration and discovery, thrill and thought. With graduate degrees in Christian thought and the Bible, and armed with a voracious appetite for most mainstream genres, he tells stories you'll read with abandon and recommend with pride—exploring the tension of faith and doubt, spirituality and culture, belief and practice, and the gritty drama that is our collective pilgrim story.

When not putting fingers to keyboard, he loves vintage jazz vinyl, a glass of Malbec, and an epic read—preferably together. He lives in Grand Rapids with his wife, two kiddos, and rambunctious boxer-pug-terrier.

www.jabouma.com • jeremy@jabouma.com

facebook.com/jaboumabooks

twitter.com/bouma

amazon.com/author/jabouma